DATE DUE			

11569

E
ALE

Alexander, Sally
Hobart.

Maggie's whopper.

**CREEKSIDE ELEMENTARY SCHOOL
MORENO VALLEY CA**

MAGGIE'S WHOPPER

Sally Hobart Alexander

Illustrated by Deborah Kogan Ray

Macmillan Publishing Company
New York

Maxwell Macmillan Canada
Toronto

Maxwell Macmillan International
New York Oxford Singapore Sydney

Macmillan Publishing Company, 866 Third Avenue, New York, NY 10022

Maxwell Macmillan Canada, Inc., 1200 Eglinton Avenue East, Suite 200, Don Mills, Ontario M3C 3N1

First edition   Printed in Hong Kong   10 9 8 7 6 5 4 3 2 1

The text of this book is set in 15 pt. Meridien. The illustrations are rendered in watercolor and watercolor pencil.

Library of Congress Cataloging-in-Publication Data
Alexander, Sally Hobart.
Maggie's Whopper / Sally Hobart Alexander; illustrated by Deborah Kogan Ray. — 1st ed.   p.   cm.
Summary: Seven-year-old Maggie sacrifices a prize fish she caught to save her great-uncle Ezra from a
hungry bear.
ISBN 0-02-700201-2
[1. Fishing — Fiction. 2. Great-uncles — Fiction. 3. Bears — Fiction.] I. Ray, Deborah Kogan, ill.
II. Title. PZ7.A3779Mag   1992   [E] — dc20   91-7726

*To the Lady of the Lake and Captain Greenwood,
Margaret and Tom Chapman, with love.*

— S.H.A.

Maggie fished from the boat, watching the lake wash against the sandy beach. She had learned to swim and fish right there, at Mosswood Lake.

"This year I'll show Tom, Uncle Ezra. I'll catch a big fish, a real whopper!"

"No doubt, Mags," he said, tugging her braid.

"Then you can take a picture, and I can hang it next to Tom's photographs of all his whoppers."

Uncle Ezra smiled. "Remember, your brother is eleven. He's had four more years to catch those fish than you, Mags."

Maggie raised her chin. "I'll catch one!" she declared, reeling in her line.

As they motored to another part of the lake, Maggie looked at the brightly colored fall leaves. She loved spending weekends with her great-uncle—in spite of the black bear, Old Thatch. He lived somewhere in the forest surrounding the lake. Uncle Ezra said the bear wasn't dangerous because he kept his distance from people. Still, Maggie trembled just thinking about him.

Uncle Ezra dropped anchor near the waterfall, where the kingfisher nested. It was there that Maggie had first seen Thatch, scratching himself on a birch tree. She had been far away in Uncle Ezra's boat, but still scared. "He's looking at us!" she had cried.

Uncle Ezra had said, "Don't worry, Mags. He's after the fish, not us."

Maggie baited her hook and tried to forget about the shaggy beast.

After an hour they moved to a cove fringed with fern.
Maggie remembered seeing Thatch there, too, eating
blueberries from the patch. When she had cried out then,
Uncle Ezra had only said, "Thatch wants to eat berries, Mags,
not us."

Maggie cast out her line and stopped thinking about the bear. She had to catch that whopper!

But when her uncle put down his fishing rod several hours later, Maggie had caught nothing big enough to keep.

"I'll catch one tomorrow," she said as they headed back, passing the lake's two other cottages.

From the dock Maggie saw something move in the forest. "Look!" she said, stiffening. "I think I see Thatch."

Uncle Ezra stepped out of the boat. "Nothing there now, sorry to say. Haven't seen that old hulk since winter. I'm afraid he might have died."

Then they would be safe, Maggie thought. But Mosswood Lake was Thatch's home, too. Even though the bear scared her, she wasn't sure she wanted him to die. Maggie squinted into the forest. "Do you really think he's dead?"

Her uncle smiled. "He's an old man, Mags, like me."

Maggie stared at her uncle's bald head and wrinkly face. "You're not that old," she said, and slipped her hand into his.

As Maggie set the table, she watched her uncle out of the corner of her eye. Uncle Ezra whistled while he put a blueberry pie into the oven. He didn't act old. And Maggie couldn't believe that Thatch was dead.

After supper they played dominoes. Next to a whopper, Maggie longed for a win. So far she hadn't beaten Uncle Ezra. When he got the double six, she said, "You always start first, but I'll whip you, anyway!"

She didn't, not the first or the second game. During the third, Uncle Ezra dozed.

He *was* old, Maggie realized, more than eighty. If Thatch could die from old age, Uncle Ezra probably could, too.

Just then he woke up, played his last domino, and won game three.

"I'll win the next one," Maggie declared.

"How 'bout a walk first?"

Maggie grabbed her jacket while Uncle Ezra took the blueberry pie from the oven. He placed it on the windowsill to cool.

"We can have some before bed?" Maggie asked.

"You bet!"

In the moonlight, they hiked down the dirt road that ran around the lake. The air smelled damp and woodsy.

After a while, Maggie heard something rustle. Uncle Ezra gave her a flashlight.

Snap! Maggie saw two deer, a doe and a fawn, their startled eyes wide with fright. In an instant they leaped away. Maggie squeezed Uncle Ezra's hand.

"Deer are all around this time of night, Mags," he said. "Let's keep the light off and listen for more."

On the way home Maggie strained her ears, hearing nothing more than their own footsteps. But just outside the cabin she heard a scraping sound. She snapped on the light. It was Thatch. He had clawed open the screen to get the blueberry pie.

Thatch grunted.

"Hurry, but don't run," warned Uncle Ezra as they headed for the cabin.

Behind the locked door of the porch, Maggie heard Thatch amble away. Her legs were so weak that she stumbled against her uncle. "He's huge!"

"Three hundred pounds, I'll bet," Uncle Ezra said, carrying her inside. "Try to forget Thatch now, and hop into bed."

"I've never seen him that close!" Maggie said.

"Neither have I, Mags. I guess it's getting harder for him to find food as he gets older. And it doesn't help that so much of the forest is being cut down." Her uncle frowned as he patted her on the head. "Shall I stay till you fall asleep?"

Maggie nodded and climbed into bed.

"Well, there's one thing we can count on, Mags. Thatch doesn't like getting close to us any more than we like it."

Maggie closed her eyes. It was good that Thatch was alive, but no matter what Uncle Ezra said, she couldn't help worrying.

At dawn the next day, Maggie and Uncle Ezra stepped into the boat. They carried a bucket of minnows for the fish and a cooler of sandwiches and cider.

Maggie fished all morning and all afternoon. A breeze blew small ripples across the water, making lapping sounds along the bank. Usually she loved to hear these sounds, but today they only made her more jumpy.

When it was time to go, Maggie still had nothing big enough to keep. "I'll show Tom yet," she said.

"That's the spirit," Uncle Ezra said.

Back in the cabin, Maggie set up the dominoes while her uncle started supper.

"Maybe I'll catch that whopper from the dock," she called, grabbing her fishing rod.

"Bait your hook now," Uncle Ezra said. "I'll bring the bucket of minnows when I come down."

The water around the dock was a mirror, reflecting the sunset and the trees. Above the lake the mountains rose and overlapped. Maggie thought there could never be a prettier picture.

Suddenly the dock bounced. Maggie scrambled to her feet and turned.

"Wow! Uncle Ezra!" She laughed in relief. "I thought you were Thatch."

Her uncle didn't smile. "Thatch is only dangerous if he thinks someone wants his food. Then he'll fight."

"And he won't lose," Maggie said.

Her uncle nodded. "Here, take some more minnows. I'll keep the bucket." He walked up the mossy slope, then settled into a chair and opened his book.

Maggie waved and cast her line back into the water. After a while, she felt a tug.

"Uncle Ezra, come! I think I caught something."

Maggie reeled in the fish as fast as she could. When it broke through the water, her heart sprang to her throat. It was a giant, speckled on top and rainbow-colored underneath. A trout, she thought, definitely a whopper, bigger than any Tom had ever caught.

Maggie continued reeling and called to her uncle, "Help me get this giant off the line!"

But Uncle Ezra did not come. Maggie turned to see what was keeping him. She nearly dropped her rod, fish and all. Uncle Ezra was dozing again, and Thatch was trudging straight toward the minnows.

Just then her uncle awoke. Maggie saw his fear and tried to think of what to do. Thatch was after the minnows—food, right beside her uncle. How could she draw him away? As the fish flopped on the hook and hit her leg, she remembered her uncle's words, "He's after the fish, not us."

Inching off the dock, she grabbed her wriggling fish and yanked it from the hook. She walked cautiously toward Thatch, getting as close as she dared. With all her might, she threw the fish past Uncle Ezra, just at Thatch's feet.

The bear paused, reared up slowly, and sniffed the air. He dropped to all fours, bent down to the trout, and sniffed again. Then he looked back at the minnows, and Uncle Ezra, even at Maggie. Which meal would he choose?

Thatch scooped the fish into his mouth with his powerful claws and lumbered toward the forest. Maggie bolted to her uncle's side. "Hurry, but don't run," she whispered, taking his elbow and picking up the bucket of minnows.

Maggie slammed the porch door. Uncle Ezra hugged her tightly and sank into a chair. "I'm sorry, Mags. I never dreamed Thatch would come so close to us. But you finally caught your whopper!"

She smiled. She really had.

"Hope you don't mind throwing away a prize fish to rescue an old man. Not sure that's a fair exchange."

Rescue? She had! She had saved his life.

"It's fair," said Maggie, taking her uncle's hand. Then she looked at him. "You have to tell the other families."

He nodded. "If they're careful with their food, maybe Thatch will play by the rules and hunt, not steal. And I sure won't take any more chances."

Maggie glanced out at the lake in the twilight and remembered her trout. She had plenty of time to catch another whopper. And what a story she'd have for Tom.

She turned to Uncle Ezra and smiled. "Let's play dominoes."